Carly's DRAGON DAYS

FIRE-BREATHERS' SCIENCE FAIR

by Tina Gagliardi

illustrated by Patrick Girouard

Science Fair NEXT WEEK!

magic Wagon

visit us at www.abdopublishing.com

Published by Magic Wagon, a division of the ABDO Group, 8000 West 78th Street, Edina, Minnesota 55439.
Copyright © 2009 by Abdo Consulting Group, Inc. International copyrights reserved in all countries. All rights reserved. No part of this book may be reproduced in any form without written permission from the publisher.

Looking Glass Library™ is a trademark and logo of Magic Wagon.

Printed in the United States.

Text by Tina Gagliardi
Illustrations by Patrick Girouard
Edited by Nadia Higgins and Jill Sherman
Interior layout and design by Nicole Brecke
Cover design by Nicole Brecke

Library of Congress Cataloging-in-Publication Data

Gagliardi, Tina.
Fire-breathers' science fair / by Tina Gagliardi ; illustrated by Patrick Girouard.
    p. cm. — (Carly's dragon days)
ISBN 978-1-60270-596-8
[1. Dragons—Fiction.] I. Girouard, Patrick, ill. II. Title.
PZ7.G1242Fir 2009
[E]—dc22
                                              2008035317

Carly seemed like an ordinary third-grade dragon at Fire-Breathers' Academy. But the truth was she was quite a bit different from her classmates. She rarely enjoyed the things they did, such as hiding treasure or fighting knights. Instead, she often played with Gretchen, her imaginary human friend.

One day at school, Carly and Gretchen were whispering when Abigail rudely interrupted them. "Carly loves humans. Carly loves humans," she chanted.

"Just ignore her," said Gretchen. "She's just jealous because her imaginary friend is a pinecone."

Carly smiled. She knew Gretchen was the best imaginary friend anyone could have.

I n class, Mrs. Longhorn made an announcement.

"Next week, Fire-Breathers' is having a science fair. I want each of you to do a project. Your work will be graded."

Carly and Gretchen looked at each other. This was going to be fun!

That evening during dinner, Carly and Gretchen talked about the project. Carly's 23 older brothers and sisters paid no attention to them at all.

"What about a moving dragon skeleton?" suggested Gretchen.

"Or a superstrong magnet!" Carly offered.

The friends came up with more great ideas. The only problem was, they couldn't figure out how to actually do any of them.

Carly and Gretchen went back to Carly's room.

"Let's see what supplies you already have," said Gretchen. "Maybe that will give us a good idea."

Gretchen dove into Carly's closet. She pulled out paints, glue, clay, and paintbrushes. Then she found a whole sheet of heart stickers. The friends spent the rest of the evening making valentines, even though it was only October.

The next day, Gretchen brought a big bag of supplies to school. She started emptying everything onto Carly's desk. Gretchen was just pulling out some glitter glue when Mrs. Longhorn said, "Test time, everyone!"

Carly frantically searched her messy desk for a pencil.

"Unprepared again, Carly?" sighed Mrs. Longhorn. The teacher pulled a pencil from behind one of her horns and handed it to Carly.

Abigail snickered. "I thought an imaginary friend was supposed to *help you!*" she said.

Carly sighed. She knew that Gretchen was not messy on purpose. Her friend just got carried away sometimes.

The whole time Carly took her test, Gretchen sat thinking.

"Carly!" Gretchen shouted. "I just had the greatest idea for your science fair project! Let's make a dragon head that shoots pretend fire! We can use baking soda and vinegar for the fire."

Carly loved the idea. She and Gretchen worked on the project every day after school. The dragon head turned out great!

On the morning of the science fair, Carly carefully packed the head in a cardboard box. In class, she asked Gretchen to look after it.

At first, Gretchen took her duty very seriously. But then Abigail's pointy dragon tail was wiggling under Carly's desk. Gretchen couldn't resist giving it just one little tickle.

Abigail jumped. *Bang!* The powerful dragon tail slammed against Carly's box.

Just then, Mrs. Longhorn called, "Science fair time, everyone!" Carly picked up the box and ran to the gym.

Slowly, Carly opened the box flaps. Her beautiful dragon head looked like a smooshed grape with eyeballs!

"Sorry!" Gretchen said.

Carly didn't know what to say.

From behind her, Carly could hear someone laughing.

"The imaginary friend strikes again!" Abigail teased.

Carly glared at Gretchen. "I can't believe you ruined my project! Maybe Abigail's right. You are too much trouble! I'd be better off if you just went away!"

With that, Gretchen vanished.

Carly went back to the classroom. She sat at her desk and waited for the other students to return.

Abigail came in to get a pencil from her desk. "Oh," she said, "I guess you decided not to hand in the smooshed grape."

Carly wished she could think of a good comeback. *Gretchen would know what to say,* she thought.

That night at dinner, Carly didn't say a word. None of her 23 brothers and sisters noticed.

If only Gretchen were here, Carly thought.

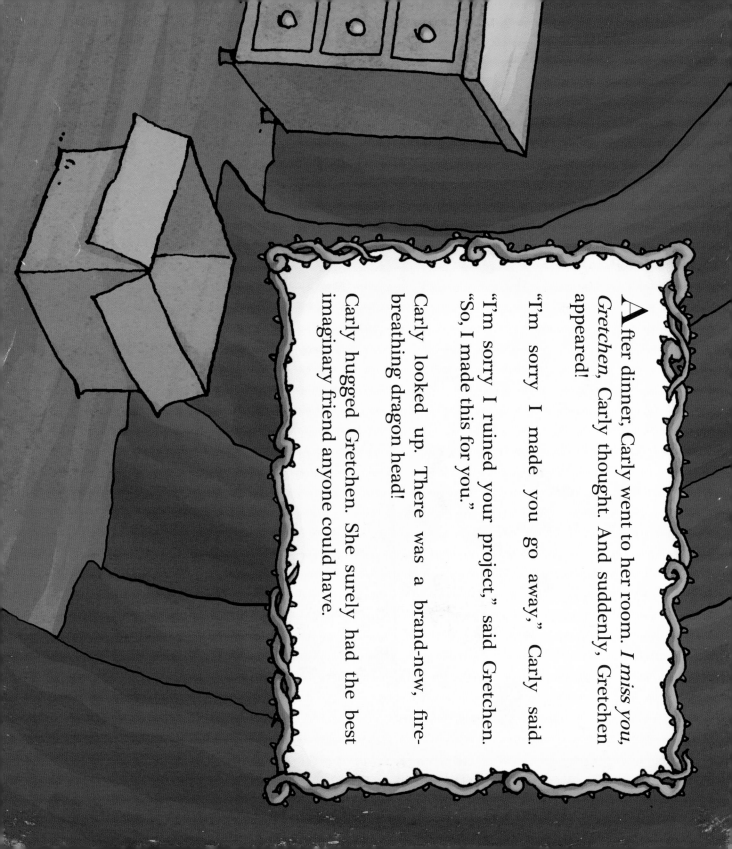

After dinner, Carly went to her room. *I miss you, Gretchen*, Carly thought. And suddenly, Gretchen appeared!

"I'm sorry I made you go away," Carly said.

"I'm sorry I ruined your project," said Gretchen. "So, I made this for you."

Carly looked up. There was a brand-new, fire-breathing dragon head!

Carly hugged Gretchen. She surely had the best imaginary friend anyone could have.

W hat do you recall from Carly's Dragon Days?

1. Why does Carly think Grethen is such a good friend?

2. How many brothers and sisters does Carly have?

3. Why did Carly get in trouble in class?

4. What does Carly make for her science project?

5. Why does Carly get mad at Gretchen?

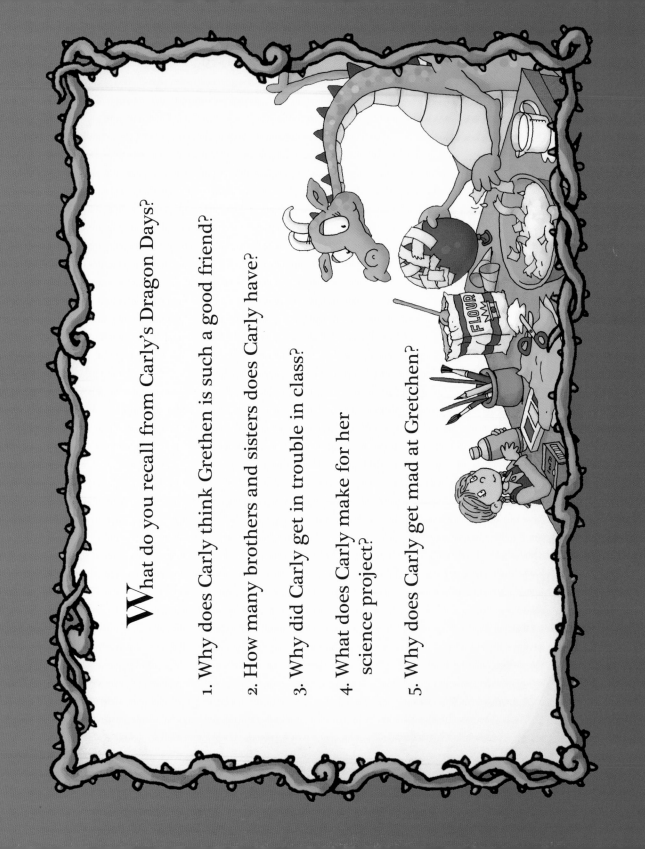